COSCOM
ENTERTAINMENT

ALSO BY A.P. FUCHS

BLOOD OF MY WORLD TRILOGY

DISCOVERY OF DEATH
MEMORIES OF DEATH
LIFE OF DEATH

UNDEAD WORLD TRILOGY

BLOOD OF THE DEAD
POSSESSION OF THE DEAD
REDEMPTION OF THE DEAD

THE AXIOM-MAN™ SAGA
(LISTED IN READING ORDER)

AXIOM-MAN or
AXIOM-MAN: TENTH YEAR ANNIVERSARY
SPECIAL EDITION
EPISODE NO. 0: FIRST NIGHT OUT
DOORWAY OF DARKNESS
EPISODE NO. 1: THE DEAD LAND
CITY OF RUIN
EPISODE NO. 2: UNDERGROUND CRUSADE
OUTLAW
EPISODE NO. 3: RUMBLINGS
FROZEN STORM (SIDE ADVENTURE)
OF MAGIC AND MEN (COMIC BOOK)
SCARLET SYNERGY (SIDE ADVENTURE)

MECH APOCALYPSE

MECH APOCALYPSE

OTHER FICTION

A STRANGER DEAD
A RED DARK NIGHT
APRIL (WRITING AS PETER FOX)
MAGIC MAN (DELUXE CHAPBOOK)
THE WAY OF THE FOG (THE ARK OF LIGHT VOL. 1)
DEVIL'S PLAYGROUND (WITH KEITH GOUVEIA)
ON HELL'S WINGS (WITH KEITH GOUVEIA)
ZOMBIE FIGHT NIGHT: BATTLES OF THE DEAD
MAGIC MAN PLUS 15 TALES OF TERROR
UNDENIABLE
THE DANCE OF MERVO AND FATHER CLOWN
FLASH ATTACK: THRILLING STORIES OF TERROR,
ADVENTURE, AND INTRIGUE
GIGANTI-GATOR DEATH MACHINE: TRIPLE FEATURE

ANTHOLOGIES (AS EDITOR)

DEAD SCIENCE
ELEMENTS OF THE FANTASTIC
VICIOUS VERSES AND REANIMATED RHYMES: ZANY ZOMBIE
POETRY FOR THE UNDEAD HEAD
METAHUMANS VS THE UNDEAD
BIGFOOT TERROR TALES VOL. 1 (WITH ERIC S. BROWN)
BIGFOOT TERROR TALES VOL. 2 (WITH ERIC S. BROWN)
METAHUMANS VS WEREWOLVES

AXIOM-MAN™
CRIMSON CLOAK
SCARLET SYNERGY

by

A.P. FUCHS

COSCOM ENTERAINMENT
WINNIPEG

ISBN 978-1-927339-91-6

Published by Coscom Entertainment

Text set in Garamond
Printed and bound in the USA

Cover art by Justin Shauf
Cover design by A.P. Fuchs

This is for Frank Dirscherl, who brought me into the world of pulp heroes and who first got me publishing superhero fiction.

Axiom-Man™
Crimson Cloak
Scarlet Synergy

Chapter One

THE CLOUDS OF smoke glowed in hues of red and orange from the raging fires beneath them in certain parts of the city. The riots started a couple of weeks ago. There was no lead-up. No triggering event. They simply started. Gradual at first. Looters breaking windows and stealing electronics. Standard stuff from a criminal point of view but, it seemed, once it was known the looters were getting away with it because the cops couldn't keep up, others joined in and the escalation began. Dumpster fires. Burning buildings. Crowds of people wandering the streets like packs of wolves searching for their prey. Men and women were beaten. Sometimes even children.

Axiom-man stood atop the old Bank of Montreal building overlooking downtown, those glowing clouds of black smoke and the stench of burning rubber reminding him of that awful night when the Doorway of Darkness opened.

It was that doorway that started it all.

All the evil.

No, Axiom-man thought. *The Doorway was only a part of it. A big part, but still just a part. It was Redsaw who opened the door, and he's out there, somewhere, and I can't find him.*

Worse, there was no proof Redsaw was behind the riots. Only rumors. Ideas of a caped shadow figure prompting those prone to destruction to carry out their passion.

Axiom-man had been at it all night and the best he was able to offer was crowd control. Some thugs got punched, others kicked, and a few intimidated by warning shots from the energy beams that blasted from his eyes.

But actually stopping the madness? It couldn't be done. Axiom-man's powers gave him an edge over the police, sure, but he wasn't lightning fast and couldn't be everywhere at once.

There was a time when things were simple. A time where all it took was a routine patrol and stopping crime where it was spotted. Then Redsaw arrived and everything changed.

Axiom-man crouched, his legs fatigued from all the running around and kicking deadbeats. He took a deep breath. Control. Self-control. Master your body.

He needed this night to be over . . . but what kind of hero thinks like that?

"Maybe you're no hero," Axiom-man said quietly. There was this idea that heroes solved every problem. That they stopped every slash at the law and put criminals in their place. There was this idea of a watchful protector overlooking each and every life the city held. At least, that's what the newspapers said. Even while walking the streets as Gabriel Garrison, Axiom-man overheard people affirming the Cobalt Crusader's efforts and how it was wonderful to know he was out there. The notion brought some comfort but not enough.

There had to be a way. How did the cops of old handle this stuff? Axiom-man thought back to the early days of the city. The days when beat cops walked the streets and straightened people out when needed. Old town Winnipeg. Small, at the time, with much less ground to cover. Somehow those guys were able to guard the streets without powers or a mask. For a moment, Axiom-man wondered if at some point in Winnipeg's past there was a secret vigilante who helped out from the shadows when needed. If the person had been overt, their record would be all over the history books. No, if there was someone, they kept it a secret as did anyone they encountered.

The fires raged. The first responders were occupied helping the wounded. Firefighters were busy putting out blazes where they could. The cops were filling holding cells with rioters.

Despite all that, Winnipeg had seen worse.

But Redsaw. Axiom-man was certain his dark counterpart was behind the violence. He just couldn't prove it, and even if he could, what could the cops do? Redsaw had yet to be captured since he appeared all that time ago. There was no way to know how strong he was now and even if the fortified cells at the downtown Special Forces station could hold him.

Axiom-man flew off the ledge and headed toward one of the fires. When he arrived on scene . . . he was too late. All that was left was a small burning locksmith shop with scorched corpses hanging out the doorway and smashed window frames.

About to leap back into the sky, Axiom-man glanced up and a glimpsed of a wisp of thick, black cloud in his right peripheral. Grimacing, he immediately darted after it. When he rounded the corner of the burning shop, he furiously waved his hand in front of his face to dispel the smoke for a clearer view. The black cloud just hovered there, a two-foot-wide mass of dense fog.

It began to glow red.

CHAPTER TWO

THROUGH A LENS of red light, the Crimson Cloak crouched on the fire escape and waited. He spent most nights like this: waiting. Though crime was tough in Muddy Waters—a nickname for Winnipeg—it wasn't a constant. The Crimson Cloak had seen to that. Ten years of long nights of lurking in the shadows, waiting, watching, intervening where and when necessary. About twenty feet up on the fire escape, he had a bird's eye view of everything. Most people didn't consider twenty feet that high, but when one climbed that high up, the ground was a lot farther below than expected. From here, he could see the entire alley. From here, he could see the street beyond, the occasional person crossing the alley on a midnight stroll. So far, there had been five people: one couple, one elderly lady, another a young lad who appeared in his mid-twenties, and a woman with a white fur coat. Probably fox.

The Crimson Cloak took a deep breath through the dark red respirator over his mouth and adjusted the near-maroon fedora on his head. Through the goggles he wore, he saw clearly in the night, their lenses tuned to amplifying all available light sources to the point of even illuminating the shadows.

This city couldn't hide from him. His eyes of fury were everywhere.

A loud low clatter of metal slamming into metal caught the Crimson Cloak's attention. He scanned the alley, but the sound did not emanate from here. It clattered again—there—across the street. The Crimson Cloak leaped down from the fire escape, large pouches carved into his cloak and cape catching the wind as he descended, slowing his arrival to the ground. He stood straight, adjusted his black tie over his black button-down and tugged at the wide collars of his overcoat. He made a straight line out of the mouth of the alley, sprinted across the street, and arrived at the alley beyond.

The loud crash, this time more precise, as if whatever had struck the metal was done in a direct manner.

It sounded again.

"Hand it over," a hurried yet firm male voice said.

"Sir, if you would just—" The sound rang again, and the Crimson Cloak noticed a baseball bat returning to a man's side just behind. To his left was a dumpster. The bat lashed out like a whip, whacking the dumpster in an echoing, low, metallic thunk.

"Hurry up, I ain't got all night," the man said.

How come it's always the same story, the Crimson Cloak thought. *Someone's out, minding their own business, going about their happy or sad day then WHAM, some tough guy in a thick jacket comes along and ruins it. And it's always about money. Always.*

The Crimson Cloak took precise steps toward his prey. The man with the bat had his back to him and as long as the panicking man crouched on the ground didn't say anything, this would be quick work.

The man swung the baseball bat again and the metal sang. Soon, any passersby might stop and the mystery of the Crimson Cloak would be revealed.

Ten years of invisibility down the drain, round and round she goes, swirling into oblivion.

The Crimson Cloak eyed the hand with the bat. It was the man's only *truly* active limb. Any gestures done with the other hand or even the shuffling of feet weren't a concern. It was about taking away their weapons.

Sometimes that meant disabling the body, but with guys like these, tough guys who were only tough with an intimidating instrument—they only had one weapon and that was the limb holding the armament.

The Cloak knew that to the man, the alley was almost as black as pitch. He didn't have red fire to help him see.

It was simple.

The Cloak silently drew up to the man and in one fluid motion slid his left hand down the arm holding the bat while simultaneously wrapping the crux of his elbow around the man's throat. He asserted the man's hand in a downward position so the bat could not be used then closed the arm, cutting off the assailant's air.

The man on the ground did not say a word as the Crimson Cloak slowly lowered the thug to the ground. After, the Cloak stood and asked, "What did he want?" He kept his voice low, just above a whisper. It was the only voice he knew after all these years. He barely spoke with a full tone to anyone, even in his other life without the cloak.

"What they always want," the man said with a groan as he got to his feet. "Stuff that doesn't belong to them."

The Crimson Cloak said nothing.

The man stared at him.

The two men remained eye to eye, the Cloak watching from behind the red lenses how the other fellow was trying to search him out, trying to read him. The Cloak knew enough to remain motionless and not say a word.

"They say the devil haunts these streets." The man's voice was a rasp. "Guess I found him." He let out a momentary chuckle. "Guess he found me." The man put his hands in his pockets. "Thanks," he said as he walked past. The Crimson Cloak could tell by the man's choppy breathing the panic hadn't worn off just yet. The man reached the mouth of the alley. The Crimson Cloak still stood there.

The man turned around and glanced over his shoulder. "Funny thing: The devil doesn't do anything nice for nobody."

Sometimes, the Crimson Cloak thought. He knew the guy in front of him knew well enough to not mention the incident.

"Say," the man said, "why don't you—" Immediately his eyes went wide, the whites overpowering the irises in a bright halo. Blood shot forth from a line across his neck. It happened so fast the Cloak only caught sight of the assailant fleeing around the corner of the building, out of sight. Out of—

The man he'd just saved dropped to his knees then fell face forward to the ground.

Six men filled the alley, three coming in from each side. All of them were armed with knives, chains, and one gun.

One weapon. Knives and chains were merely extensions of a person's arm. A gun was different. A gun could project.

The Crimson Cloak remained calm and slowly raised his hands to his neck and loosened his tie.

"Look-ee-loo," said one fella. "The devil is real and he's nervous."

The Crimson Cloak undid the Windsor knot and pulled the tie down from around his neck.

"We strip teasing now?" the guy said.

Keep talkin', bub. Keep talkin'.

The six men advanced; not too quick, not too slow. Their arms bent at the elbow, biceps tensing, and their fingers curled into fists that reaffirmed their holds on the knives and chains.

The gun.

The Cloak let his tie drop to his right hand and held on. The tie was made of some sort of elastic material that could extend but then retract back to its original shape.

One knife started in on the left. The Cloak blocked the swing and delivered a deft right hook to the man's jaw, sending him stumbling back. Another came in from the right and was quickly dispatched with a steel-toed kick to the solar plexus. He dropped, cradling his middle, arm around the ribs.

The man who first attacked came in again: left, right, left, right, like a boxer just throwing out everything he had. The Cloak dodged the majority of the blows but one caught him in the neck. He coughed into his respirator, utilizing its simple tech to take in more oxygen than normal. This helped make the blow to the neck easier to take. Left, right, left—block. Another hook then an uppercut then a full-body-powered hook to the man's ear, the Cloak spinning around to complete the blow. His deep red cape spun with him, temporarily blinding the other four, the man with the gun being of the most concern. The Cloak searched for him as the men took a second to wipe their eyes after the fabric no doubt brushed over their eyelids.

The Crimson Cloak got in between two of them and jumped up, kicked out, nailing both guys in the chest, his feet connecting where heart and ribcage met. The second the Cloak's feet hit the pavement, he grabbed the men by the hair and did a spin to disorient them then clocked one in the nose and another between the eyes.

The gunman raised his weapon. All he did was cock the hammer, the sound enough to make everybody stop.

All these men were cowards if the sound of a gun getting ready was enough to shake them. But the gunman had this look in his eyes. He knew what he was holding. He knew he held the power of Life and Death and his trigger was the balance beam.

The Cloak brought his hands in behind his cape, hiding them.

The gun was aimed straight at him. "Are we done?"

The Cloak remained silent.

"I said are we done!" the man shouted.

Strong arms wrapped themselves around the Cloak's legs, squeezing like a pair of bolas, and pulled him to the ground. A hefty guy was on top of him in no time. The fists came down. The Crimson Cloak raised his forearms like a wall in front of his face, blocking some of the shots, others coming through. His respirator was solid, made of metal, and took most of the blows, but it hurt like hell when each punch forced the thing into the tissue and bone of his face.

With his right hand, the Cloak took his tie, draped it over the man's wrists when both of them came down with fists, then like lightning, pulled the tie under the man's wrists and spun it around them a couple of times, disabling him. The Cloak angled his leg and delivered a hard knee into the small of the man's back then one shot with each knee into each of the man's kidneys. It was enough to jostle the guy off him.

The man with gun took a shot. The Crimson Cloak didn't move. Neither did the gunman.

The shot was a warning.

The Cloak hated warnings unless he was the one giving them.

A fist caught him in the cheek. He should have been more aware and it was right then that ten years of nights suddenly felt like twenty. Was he getting too slow for this? Not as observant?

The Cloak lashed out with all he had and took the guy down to the ground with a bear hug then hammered down on him at least a dozen times if not more.

"Stop!" The hammer cocked again.

The Cloak saw his tie laying on the ground like a coiled snake, the hands it once bound now free and coming for him. The Cloak dove beneath them, the blow missing him, and he snatched the tie from the ground then snapped it out like a whip, cracking it against the hand holding the gun. The man didn't let go of the weapon but his fingers dipped to the side. The Cloak swung out his leg along the ground and swept the man's legs out from under him.

Another shot.

"Mike, stop!" one of the guys said. "Johnny had it comin'. He knew not to go solo. The cape here, he—"

The Cloak kicked him in the chin with his heel, silencing him. "Don't allude to me."

The man groaned on the ground just as "Mike" sprinted past. The Cloak tried to sting him with his tie but missed, and so the chase was on.

The Crimson Cloak dug in deep and ran out of the alley, quickly checked both ways, spotted the guy, then ran along the buildings' walls as close to the shadows as possible. He was gaining ground quickly and it brought a smile to his face. Maybe ten years of nights hadn't beaten him after all?

Reaching into his pocket, the Cloak focused his eyes at the base of the man's neck. He pulled out a baseball, hard, solid. *Good night.* He hurled the ball through the air. Mike's head snapped back and his legs folded under him as he hit the ground.

The Cloak thought of the baseball. *Let some kid keep it as a souvenir.* He was gloved anyway so fingerprints weren't an issue. Grimacing, the Crimson Cloak grabbed the man by his jacket and dragged him into another alley. With as much force as he could muster, he slammed the man up against the rough brick wall.

"I'm done with kids like you," the Cloak said.

The man was only partially coherent after that hit with the ball. His eyes nearly rolled to the back of his head and the Cloak wasn't sure the man was even still with it. The Cloak let him drop into his arms . . . then drew his face close to Mike's.

"Scream."

———

Mike's legs melted in terror as the auburn mist surrounded him, seeming to suck him out of the alley. He dropped to his knees. His arms went numb and his heart raced so hard his pulse was in his temples. He wanted to scream but every time he tried, the scream was directed inward, rattling his bones and making his lungs hurt.

Breathe.

Just breathe.

But no air came. Not in this place of muddy red mist.

There was no sound either.

Just then a shadow materialized in the mist and seized him. This humanoid shadow figure grabbed him by the shoulders and yanked him to his feet. Mike tried to get away but each effort to unhook the shadow figure's hands from his shoulders only made the thing grip him even tighter.

A scream.

All he wanted was to scream and let out the panic boiling inside. But like all efforts to expel sound, nothing came out of his mouth.

Did he just die and this place was the afterlife? Was he on his way to hell as the shadow figure pulled him farther and farther into the mist?

A black rectangle materialized. It was a few meters long and a couple meters high. It had wheels. Some kind of paddy wagon?

The grip on his shoulders tightened even more.

He gasped as he was thrown into the rectangle and landed hard inside it. The rectangle slid shut with a violent slam and Mike suddenly found himself in pitch darkness.

Heart still hammering, he tried to catch his breath, however each effort to get himself under control only made things worse. His chest tightened and his throat sealed shut.

More panic.

More fear.

His heart pounded even harder and with his numb arms, he was certain he was having a heart attack.

The pitch black surrounding him began to fade and the fiery red came back into view. At first it was a pleasant relief from the dark but soon the mist seemed to shine even brighter, and he wished things would go dark again. He closed his eyes but the red light was too bright and everything was a bright orange through his eyelids.

Breathe.

Just breathe.

Another shadowy figure emerged, this one charging at him. Once it reached him, it jerked him to his feet and wrapped its arms around him. The more Mike struggled against its hold, the harder the shadow squeezed.

Another rectangle appeared, the same as the first, and, like before, Mike was thrown inside it and a door slammed shut, sealing him in the dark.

His thoughts scattered and once more he thought he had died.

Fragments.

Images.

A little boy no more than five thrown into the wagon.

A little girl the same age thrown into the wagon.

It was then Mike understood: he was being judged. By whom or by what, he couldn't recall, and once more he thought he had died and this was the Almighty's way of punishing him.

The wagon dematerialized around him and once more he found himself in the thick of crimson mist.

A flash of blue fluttered somewhere ahead.

Voices.

Sound.

The blue again.

Then the light went out and he was back in the alley. As his eyes adjusted to the dark, he saw two men in capes in front of him. He knew one of them. The man of legend. The Crimson Cloak. The other—he had no idea.

His arms were still numb and his eyes hurt from all that red light.

He tried to get up to run but both his legs were like over-boiled spaghetti, and he got the mental picture of noodles for legs instead of muscle and bone.

Breathe.

He could breathe!

He sat there on the cold stone ground, catching his breath with tears running down his cheeks.

He was alive . . .

. . . and in trouble.

Chapter Three

Moments earlier . . .

THE CRIMSON CLOAK held the man by the collar of his jacket, red mist and smoke emanating from somewhere within the man's red cape.

The thick red mist filled the alley.

Just then a blur of blue danced on the left. The Crimson Cloak looked. It was a man in a costume. A blue costume that consisted of dark blue pants that blended into boots of the same color, with a brighter blue slash going at a diagonal across his chest, and his arms the same dark blue as his pants. He wore light blue gloves and had a gold triangle for a belt buckle. His face was hidden beneath a mask, which had its own light blue material traveling at an angle across his face. Tufts of brown hair parted in the middle stuck out from the top of the mask. The man also had a light blue cape.

"Unhand him," the man said and side-kicked the Crimson Cloak.

The Cloak took the blow, his main mission to finish his time with the criminal. He would make quick work of the man in blue later.

"I said let him go!" the man in blue said.

"Quiet," the Crimson Cloak said. A split second after he said the word, arms came up from behind him, scooping him up from underneath his armpits and, pulling backward, forcing him to let go of the man.

The man in blue kept pulling the Crimson Cloak away. He didn't have time for this. The Cloak grabbed the man in blue's arms, pulled down and violently bent forward at the waist, flipping the guy over him and onto the ground.

The man who had once been lost inside the murk of red mist started to come around but the Crimson Cloak knew he was no flight risk. The menacing power of the red gas would have crippled the man with fear.

The man in blue got up off the ground and delivered a front kick aimed at the Crimson Cloak's middle. The Cloak blocked it, took a step forward, then administered a right hook to the man's face.

The man in blue raised his hands in a fighting stance, clearly ready for more. And if it was *more* he wanted, the Crimson Cloak was more than happy to oblige.

———

Axiom-man got ready and delivered a quick jab at the man in the goggled mask. How or what he had been doing to the man in the jacket with that red gaseous gunk, he didn't know. All he knew was the man in the jacket needed help. How Axiom-man ended up in this alley, he'd have to figure out later.

Axiom-man jabbed again and was blocked, so he lunged forward with a straight punch and landed it squarely on the man in the mask's chin. The blow was intended to put the man out for good but there hadn't been enough power behind the blow to do so.

Axiom-man tried to light up his eyes in an effort to scare the other costumed man but he couldn't. He tried to hover above the ground, but his feet remained glued in place.

He was without his powers.

The man in the respiratory-like mask brought his fist in from the side, clipping Axiom-man in the jaw. A kick to the ribs was enough to make Axiom-man stumble to the side.

He had to dig deep. Had to put an end to this man who was hurting someone else. Had to . . . . Crying. He looked and, sitting with her knees drawn up into her chest, was a little girl inside a black wagon.

It all came together. The man in the goggles was saving her.

Axiom-man dropped his hands. "I don't want to fight you."

"Could have fooled me," the man in the red fedora said, his hands still raised in a fighting position.

"I misread the situation. I thought you were hurting that man; that, and you're wearing a mask."

"I *was* hurting him. I was making him pay for tonight. Making him pay for past sins against . . . . He had to pay!"

More whimpering came from the wagon. Axiom-man turned to see the little girl sitting all alone, frightened. When he returned his gaze to the man in the mask, the man had lowered his arms.

"First things first," the man in the red cape said. He reached behind his back, paused a moment, then pulled out a pair of handcuffs. He went over to the man in the jacket, hoisted him up by the collar, then dragged him to a nearby streetlamp. He threw the man against it, took the man's arms and put them behind his back, and cuffed him against the lamp's pole.

"Tend to the girl while I radio this in," the man in the mask said.

Axiom-man went over to the wagon. Tears ran down the girl's face. "It's okay. I'm not going to hurt you."

She still continued to whimper.

"Shhh. It's okay. You're safe now," Axiom-man said.

He reached for her but she wouldn't move and just sat there huddled with her arms around her knees.

The man in the mask appeared beside him. "Once she's safe, you and I are going to have a little talk."

"Agreed," Axiom-man said.

Sirens rose on the air. Any moment now the police would show up and take the girl to safety.

"Meet me on the roof," the man in the mask said. He produced what looked like a grapple gun from his belt, aimed it upward, then shot the grapple over the building's ledge. The line went taut, and the man climbed along the line to the roof, red cape expanding behind him.

Why aren't my powers working? Axiom-man thought. *This is too weird. I need them, especially now that I'm, what, working with another superhero?* Thankfully, there were metal stairs on the outside of the same building so Axiom-man could get up there, too.

The girl whimpered again.

"It's going to be okay. It's going to be—" A green mist quickly surrounded him and became as thick as pea soup. It all happened so fast Axiom-man had taken a lungful before holding his breath.

What was going on?

What was . . . . He quickly got dizzy and fell to the ground. Before he closed his eyes, he saw the same green smoke coming from the roof.

———

The Crimson Cloak awoke with a pounding headache. He opened his eyes and took in his surroundings: brown leather chairs, a couch with a coffee table. Off to the side was a counter with a bunch of inboxes behind it. The floor was carpeted in a deep maroon with gold flowers printed into it. A crystal chandelier hung from the ceiling, illuminating the wood-paneled walls.

The man in blue lay off to the side, face down.

The Crimson Cloak got up and stumbled a few steps. He put his hand against the wall for balance.

Where are we? he thought.

He cleared his throat.

He reached into a pouch inside his trench coat and produced a couple painkillers. He removed the respirator enough to have access to his mouth then popped them in and swallowed.

He went over to the man in blue, crouched down, and gave him a shake. "Get up."

The man in blue stirred then blinked open his eyes. He put a hand to his head. "What happened? Where are we? The last thing I remember was green gas or smoke."

"Knockout gas," the Crimson Cloak said.

The man in blue sat up. "Why are we in a hotel lobby?"

"I don't know."

"The girl, the man . . ."

"I know. We have to assume the police came in time."

"Where am I?" the man in blue said, seemingly talking to himself.

"A lobby," the Crimson Cloak said.

"No, I mean *where* am I? I appeared in that alley after . . . after . . ." He put both palms to his temples and kept them there.

The Crimson Cloak needed answers. "Who are you?"

The man looked at him. "Axiom-man."

"And the costume?"

"It's a uniform."

"Where did you come from? I was in that alley, and you just appeared out of nowhere."

Axiom-man removed his hands from his temples. He seemed to pause and think. The Crimson Cloak knew Axiom-man was pondering how much information he was going to give up.

"In my world there are . . . thin spots," Axiom-man said.

"Thin spots?" the Cloak said.

Axiom-man nodded. "Thin spots. Black clouds that I accidentally released a long time ago. These thin spots lead to other worlds. Other Earths."

It seemed far-fetched and the Crimson Cloak wasn't buying it, yet at the same time, Axiom-man just appeared in that alley. He didn't walk in or climb down anything. He just simply showed up.

"Let's say I believe you," the Crimson Cloak said. "Why did you attack me?"

Axiom-man stood. "I saw a man in a mask doing something strange—by force—to someone who seemed completely helpless. I had to do something." Axiom-man massaged his temples a moment then dropped his arms to his sides. "What were you doing to that man?"

The Crimson Cloak smirked. "Justice. This . . . gas I use" —he brought both hands slowly to his face and gently traced his fingers around the edges of his respirator— "makes someone experience their worst fears. That man was in the midst of kidnapping that little girl. Fortunately, I was nearby and heard a tiny scream before it was abruptly cut off. He had to pay for what he was about to do."

"What's your name?" Axiom-man said.

"The Crimson Cloak."

"Friend or foe?"

"Friend, but don't take my word for it. That would be a mistake. Understand?"

Axiom-man nodded and seemed to consider his words. Anybody could say anything for any reason. "I'll be careful."

It wasn't like the Cloak to be handing out lessons but at the same time, he didn't fully trust Axiom-man. The guy could be playing possum or clueless hero. The Crimson Cloak decided to be careful. The story about the thin spots weighed on him. Other Earths? It was the first he heard of it.

Again, he had to be careful.

CHAPTER FOUR

AXIOM-MAN HAD NO choice but to hand a little trust over to this "Crimson Cloak." The man seemed to be on the up and up. He *did* save that girl, after all, unless he was trying to get her for himself. No. He couldn't let his mind go there and be paranoid about every single thing. For the time being, he'd work with the man in the dark red trench coat in figuring out how or why they wound up in a hotel lobby.

He turned to the Crimson Cloak. "Do you recognize this place? Do you know where we are?"

"You're asking the obvious. We're in a hotel lobby."

"I meant *which* hotel. Ever been here before?"

The Crimson Cloak shook his head. He glanced over at the main doors. There were no windows to the outside. The doors were made of solid oak. The Cloak went over and tugged on one of the handles. The door didn't budge. Axiom-man came over and did the same with the same result. If only he had his powers here. He could use his ultra strength and force the doors open. He did another power check, first trying to light up his eyes with crackling blue energy then tried to hover above the floor. He couldn't do either. He reached up and pulled several strands of his bangs down so he could see his hair. It was brown, not blue like it would be if his powers were activated. He tried *shifting* to turn his powers back on but to no success. It appeared that in this world, on this Earth, he was powerless. He wondered if the Crimson Cloak had any special abilities.

"I don't know how to ask this," Axiom-man said, "so I'll keep it simple: Do you have any special . . . powers?"

The Crimson Cloak waited a moment before slowly shaking his head.

"I just realized we better be careful what we say. Somebody could be listening in," Axiom-man said.

"You're right and we've probably said too much already. From now on, it's just business, the first order of which is how to get out of here."

Axiom-man examined the door handles. There wasn't any obvious locking mechanism so he assumed the doors could only be locked from the outside.

The Crimson Cloak reached to somewhere beneath his cape then produced a small cylinder.

"What's that?" Axiom-man asked.

"Explosives. I'm going to spray it around the door and blow it open." He crouched down and no sooner did he lay a six-inch bead of gray foam along the door did Axiom-man hear a cough behind them.

The two men in capes turned, and there before them was a group of ninjas, three rows deep and seven across.

The Crimson Cloak flung his cape off his shoulders and raised his hands in a fighting stance. Out of his peripheral, he saw Axiom-man do the same.

"Hope you know how to fight," the Crimson Cloak said.

"I do," Axiom-man replied.

The ninjas closed in and the first made a swing for the Crimson Cloak. The Cloak blocked the punch and delivered a one-two combo to the ninja's head then quickly swept the ninja's legs out from under him. One ninja sprung in from the side. The Crimson Cloak delivered a side kick and caught the ninja between the ribs. The ninja spun around and delivered a back kick to the Cloak's middle. Not wasting any time, the Crimson Cloak stepped forward and threw a front kick first to the ninja's chest then he re-cocked his leg and went for the head and nailed the ninja beneath the chin. The ninja fell to the ground.

Quickly, the Crimson Cloak searched for Axiom-man and saw the man in blue fighting off his attackers. Before he could offer an assist, the Cloak was toe-to-toe with another ninja. The Crimson Cloak punched the black-clad figure in the stomach then snuck a swift hook to its head. Ensuring the ninja would go down, he doubled down with a back fist to the ninja's temple and the ninja dropped to the floor.

Three down, eighteen more to go.

The Crimson Cloak grabbed each side of his cape and raised it out like wings before flapping it down as a momentary distraction while he got in between two ninjas. He delivered a front kick to one and with the same leg a back kick to the other. The ninjas staggered back. One came in with a flying side kick. The Crimson Cloak grabbed the extended leg out of the air, held on tight, then spun the ninja around into its comrade. They both hit the floor. The Cloak jumped and landed on the two ninjas' heads, his heavy boots knocking them out.

Two more down. Sixteen more to go.

Good thing he wasn't alone.

———

Axiom-man found himself surrounded. It was almost fortunate there were so many of them: They wouldn't be able to attack all at once. He saw the Crimson Cloak fight. Clearly the guy was trained in at least one martial arts discipline. Axiom-man wasn't. His fighting experience was all from street brawling, but in the end, a punch was a punch, a kick was a kick. Doing it correctly was another matter, but he must have been doing something right over the past few years otherwise he wouldn't be here now.

He did a quick count of the ninjas: Sixteen.

The Crimson Cloak struck all who came near.

Axiom-man shot a right hook to a ninja's jaw, kicked him in the arm then in the back of the knee. The ninja staggered and Axiom-man came in with another hook, dropping the ninja.

Fifteen more to go.

Axiom-man got clocked good and hard and, for a moment, his world spun and the room tilted. He lashed out, first with a right back fist then a smooth follow through with a left hook. He kicked the staggering ninja in the groin then grabbed the ninja by the head and delivered a hard knee to its face.

Fourteen to go. Maybe less, depending on how the Crimson Cloak was making out.

A kick to Axiom-man's gut made him double over. He fell to his knees but quickly scrambled to his feet. He blocked a straight punch and grabbed the ninja on either side of its head and smashed a hard head-butt to the ninja's face. The ninja dropped.

Axiom-man dodged a punch, got clipped by another, this one causing him to taste blood. He jabbed the ninja between the eyes then followed through with a straight punch to the face and a kick to the ninja's ribs. With the ninja slightly bent over, Axiom-man landed a crescent kick across the ninja's head and sent him to the floor.

Twelve to go.

—————

The Crimson Cloak was trained for this. Endless hours of kicking and boxing practice in his makeshift hideaway prepared him for this moment.

He grabbed two ninjas by the collars, brought them in close, and in a blur of motion, slammed their heads together. They went down in a heap.

Ten to go.

One came in from behind and wrapped his arm around the Cloak's throat. The Crimson Cloak elbowed him in the ribs, adjusted his stance, then tossed him over his shoulder. The moment the ninja hit the floor, the Cloak came down on his head with an axe kick, knocking him out cold.

Another ninja landed a jab on the Crimson Cloak's nose. The Cloak dodged the following punch and swept the legs out from underneath the ninja. He kicked him in the face on his way down.

The eight remaining ninjas moved in as one unit and surrounded the caped figures.

No time for mercy, the Crimson Cloak thought.

He lunged forward and landed a dual punch with one fist jabbing into the ninja's throat and the other in his face.

The Crimson Cloak glanced over at Axiom-man, who was fighting off two attackers. The Cloak moved to help him and pulled one of the ninjas away from behind. He kicked him behind the knee, put him in a headlock and rained blow after blow into the ninja's face. He dropped the ninja to the ground.

Six more to go.

The Crimson Cloak jumped into the air and did the splits, kicking two ninjas at once. Axiom-man grabbed one of them by the shoulder, spun him around so he faced him then delivered a solid right hook across the ninja's jaw.

Five.

The Crimson Cloak made quick work of two more by landing his heavy boot into the temple of one ninja and into the jaw of another.

Three.

This time there was clear hesitation in the eyes of the remaining ninjas. Two moved toward the Crimson Cloak, one toward Axiom-man. The Cloak back-fisted one then, with his palm, struck the cheekbone of the other. Out of the corner of his eye, he caught Axiom-man slamming his palms on either side of the ninja's head, nailing him in the temples. The ninja dropped.

The remaining two split off. One delivered a kick to the Crimson Cloak's middle, one so hard it gave him momentary pause. Infuriated, the Crimson Cloak punched the ninja in the chest, knocking the wind out of him. He then grabbed the ninja and tossed him over his hip but not before bringing his fist down like a hammer on top of the ninja's head.

Axiom-man wrestled with the last ninja, the two rolling on the floor. After a moment, Axiom-man was on top of the ninja and sat on his chest. The ninja flailed his arms, trying to land a shot. Axiom-man blocked each attempt then threw an open-palm strike to the ninja's nose and a follow through with a straight punch to the ninja's mouth. He hit him again and again.

The Crimson Cloak pulled Axiom-man off the ninja. "Okay, okay . . . he's done. It's over."

Axiom-man stood on visibly shaky legs, panting, clearly trying to catch his breath.

"It's over," the Crimson Cloak said again, scanning the heap of black-clad bodies. One stirred. He kicked him in the face, putting him back under, then cursed himself for not leaving at least one ninja conscious for questioning. So far, that's all they had: questions.

Why here? Why this place? Why the barrage of ninjas?

The door!

Axiom-man seemed calmer. "What was . . . that . . . all about?"

"I don't know," the Crimson Cloak said, moving toward the door.

"Still going to try and blow the thing open?" Axiom-man said.

"It's our only way out." He pulled out the small cylinder and continued its bead along the doorframe.

Once done, he set the fuse and began stepping away.

"Take cover," he told Axiom-man.

Axiom-man nodded and retreated further into the room.

The Crimson Cloak did the same.

Silently, he set the fuse and watched as it made its way to the explosive foam.

A giant bang echoed throughout the room as the thing blew into splinters, revealing a metal door behind it.

"You've got to be kidding me," Axiom-man said.

After a moment of silence, the Crimson Cloak said, "It appears that way."

A *ding* rang out behind them. They both turned to face it, first Axiom-man then the Crimson Cloak. The elevator door slid open and revealed a ninja clad in red. He stepped out and even from where he stood,

Axiom-man saw this one was about a foot taller than the ones they just faced.

"Are you serious?" Axiom-man said.

The Crimson Cloak remained silent.

The red ninja stepped out of the elevator and the door slid closed behind it. Axiom-man sensed this ninja was not like the others. It exuded a level of skill the others were missing.

"Be careful," Axiom-man said.

"I'm always careful," the Cloak said.

The ninja did not move but instead stared at them.

Discomfort set in and Axiom-man wasn't sure who was going to make the first move.

After a long moment, the red ninja slowly made his way toward them, his feet moving along the ground in complete silence.

"We don't have time for this," the Crimson Cloak said and, clenching his fists, charged at the ninja head-on.

The ninja grabbed him by the arm, spun, and flung the Crimson Cloak into the wall. The Cloak turned around and came at the ninja with a front kick and a one-two combo. The offense was blocked and he got hammered with a punch to the chest.

Not wanting to stand around, Axiom-man moved in and threw a right hook then a left. Both got blocked. He kicked the ninja in the shin while the Crimson Cloak threw a right hook and clipped the ninja across the nose.

The Cloak delivered another front kick, which was blocked, but he quickly re-cocked at the knee and threw it again, this time nailing the ninja's solar plexus. The ninja staggered back a step then closed the gap with a turning kick to the side of the Cloak's head. His hat or the bands keeping the goggles and respirator to his face must be padded, Axiom-man presumed, which was why the

Crimson Cloak didn't go down but quickly retaliated with a side kick to the ninja's ribs. Axiom-man did the same and kicked through the attempted block.

A sudden dump of adrenaline made Axiom-man feel invincible. He charged at the ninja and, after the Crimson Cloak had kicked the ninja in the chest, came at him with all he had. He thrust his forearm into the ninja's neck, his other arm against the ninja's ribs and slammed him up against the wall. He shot hook after hook and got blocked after four shots landed. The ninja grabbed him by the arm, spun him around and held him for a second with his arm wrenched behind his back.

Out of the corner of his eye, he saw the Crimson Cloak bring an axe kick down on the arm holding Axiom-man, freeing him. The Crimson Cloak delivered another axe kick, this time on the ninja's shoulder. The Cloak threw a right jab followed by a left hook and cranked the ninja's head to the side.

Axiom-man blocked a front kick then kicked the ninja square in the kneecaps, first the right then the left. He did it again and the ninja dropped to his knees.

The Crimson Cloak grabbed the ninja by the front of his suit and delivered blow after blow. The ninja slumped to the floor. The Cloak turned and took a step toward Axiom-man. The ninja reached out and grabbed the Crimson Cloak by the ankle, then, with his other arm, pressed his forearm against the back of the Cloak's leg, forcing a bend in the knee and causing him to trip. The Crimson Cloak stumbled then with a cry quickly closed the distance and delivered a low side kick to the ninja's head. The ninja fell forward and didn't move.

Heart racing, Axiom-man breathed with relief; it seemed to be over. He glanced around the room.

Unconscious ninjas littered the floor. He glanced to the door, remembering they were trapped.

CHAPTER FIVE

"ARE YOU ALL right?" Axiom-man asked.

"I'll live," the Crimson Cloak said.

A ninja stirred on the floor. The Crimson Cloak kicked it with his boot, sending it back to La La Land. *And I didn't keep one conscious for questioning again. Damn. Axiom-man's giving me an off night.*

The elevator dinged and the door slid open.

Axiom-man moved toward it, but the Crimson Cloak stopped him with a firm palm to his chest. "Don't. It's a trap."

"Was just going to check it out."

"Be my guest but be careful."

Axiom-man nodded and the Cloak kept watch.

The man in the blue cape moved slowly to the elevator doors. He peered out. "There's nothing in here."

"I'm going to try to blow the front door open again," the Crimson Cloak said.

Axiom-man stepped over and around the ninjas' bodies and joined him.

The Cloak pulled out another canister of explosive from somewhere inside his trench coat then studied the doorframe. The doorframe was metal as was the door itself, the door fused to the frame, sealed. Just as he about to spray the explosive foam around the door, a loud *whoosh* rose on his right. The entire wall went aflame. Then one couch erupted on fire then the other one. The chair went up next then the wall across the room.

The heat instantly made the Crimson Cloak sweat beneath his many layers of garments.

"Come on, let's go!" Axiom-man shouted, already near the elevators.

The Crimson Cloak grimaced then joined Axiom-man by the elevator.

"I know it's a trap, but we have no choice but to get in," Axiom-man said.

Black smoke settled down between them. Axiom-man coughed. The Crimson Cloak didn't, his respirator creating clean air for him.

The Crimson Cloak shook his head and the two entered the elevator.

The Cloak scanned the buttons and noticed they only went up. There was no lower level to this place.

He pressed the close door button. The door didn't shut. The heat from the inferno in the lobby grew more intense. He pressed the button again, this time repeatedly. Finally, the door slid shut.

"Now what?" Axiom-man asked, coughing.

"Now we wait," the Crimson Cloak said as the number 2 button lit on its own and the elevator began to move.

———

The figure sat in the dark surrounded by computer monitors.

"Interesting," he said. "Let's see how they do on Level Two."

———

The elevator came to a halt and the door slid open, revealing what looked like an abandoned aviary.

The two men remained in the elevator.

"It's no doubt a trap," Axiom-man said. "Yeah, I know, I keep saying that." He pressed the button to close the doors. Nothing happened. He pressed it again. Same thing: Nothing. He pressed it several times but the door remained open.

"Looks like we have no choice," the Crimson Cloak said.

"Looks that way."

The two men stepped out of the elevator. The door began to close. Axiom-man tried to stop it by putting his hand between the door and the frame, but no matter how hard he pulled against the closing door, he couldn't keep it open and the door closed. If only he had his ultra strength, maybe he could have prevented it from closing.

The aviary was cast in gray light. Two enormous dead trees filled the center of the room. There were walkways lined with dead trees and empty bird cages on either side.

"Don't go too far in," the Crimson Cloak said. "It's probably what whoever is doing this wants."

Axiom-man nodded. He tried the elevator call button, hoping it would open the door.

It didn't.

Have no choice but to wait and see, he thought. "So," he said, "how long have you been doing this for? The superhero thing, I mean."

"Quiet. We're probably being watched and are probably being listened to, remember?"

"Sorry." *It was a dumb question anyway.*

The minutes ticked by, each second seeming longer than the last. Whoever was behind this obviously wanted them to go further into the room.

Axiom-man took a step forward, but the Crimson Cloak stopped him with yet another palm to the chest. This was getting old.

"Wait," the Cloak said.

"Nothing is going to happen if we stay still."

"We wait."

Axiom-man sighed but understood where the Crimson Cloak was coming from.

Soon a voice broke the silence. "Help me." Female. Desperate. Coming from farther in the aviary. "Help me. I've been kidnapped."

Axiom-man turned to the Crimson Cloak. The Cloak's face was like stone.

"Help me. Please, help me."

"She needs our help," Axiom-man said quietly.

"Then we help her. But stay on guard."

Axiom-man nodded and he and the Crimson Cloak moved farther into the aviary.

"Help me."

They cautiously walked amongst the dead trees, each a gray skeleton of their former selves. Empty bird cages testified to a life long before this place was abandoned.

"Help me. Please. I'm stuck." Her words came from just ahead.

"We're close," Axiom-man said.

The Crimson Cloak remained silent. He moved with a quiet grace Axiom-man had seen only once before by someone from his world. Pure stealth. Axiom-man tried to mimic him and felt clumsy.

"Help. Please help."

The voice was louder.

They moved past the trees in the center of the room and took a path on the left.

"Help." The voice was louder now and just as desperate.

Axiom-man quickened his pace.

"Help."

He wasn't sure if he should assure the person help was on the way given the Crimson Cloak's warning of surveillance earlier. He opted to keep his mouth shut.

"Help."

Right there. Just a few feet ahead and—an old wooden chair with a rusty phonograph on it.

"Help," the phonograph said. "Help me."

"Oh crap," Axiom-man said under his breath.

The Crimson Cloak must have heard him because he replied, "Oh crap is right."

———

The Crimson Cloak chastised himself. He should have known better. All that silence only to be broken when they decided to not stick by the elevator. But he couldn't help it. His entire crusade was about helping people, even those who didn't deserve it. He couldn't blame Axiom-man for wanting to do the same thing.

"Help," the phonograph said. He picked it up and turned it off.

The room went eerily quiet.

"What was the point of that?" Axiom-man asked. Someone was trying to—before he could finish the thought, the Cloak finished it for him.

"A way to get us away from the elevator. The question is who was just here to turn this thing on?"

"Do you think they're still here?"

"Doubtful. Come on, let's go back to the elevator."

Just as they began to move, a streak of silver zipped between them.

"What the—" Axiom-man started.

Another streak went by then another and another until, "Ow." The Crimson Cloak looked and Axiom-man held his arm.

"What happened?" the Cloak asked.

Axiom-man slowly peeled his hand away from his arm. There was a four-inch-long gash on his left biceps.

Another blur of silver and Axiom-man's hand snapped to this other arm. When he took his fingers away from it, the Crimson Cloak saw it was another cut.

A streak of silver went by and the Crimson Cloak felt it strike his thick clothing. Another streak, this one across the Cloak's leg.

"You okay?" Axiom-man asked.

"I'm fine."

The Crimson Cloak listened closely. There was a flapping sound. He looked up and, there, perched on one of the branches, was a robotic bird about the size of a crow.

"Found our culprit," the Crimson Cloak said and nodded toward the bird.

Axiom-man looked. "Let's hope it's the only on—" A blur of silver came from behind the two men, zipping between them.

The Crimson Cloak reached into a pouch hidden in his cloak and pulled out a thin, metal cylinder. He snapped his wrist and extended the retractable baton. He handed it to Axiom-man and pulled out a second baton for himself. Normally, he'd use them as escrima sticks.

The robot bird left its perch and dove straight at them. The Crimson Cloak swiped at it with the baton and missed. The thing was too fast.

Whack! Axiom-man had nailed one and it lay on the floor, wings twitching.

Another one swooped in and this time the Crimson Cloak honed in on it and swung the baton, smacking the bird from mid-flight. It hit the floor. The Cloak whacked it a few times to thoroughly break it.

Another streak of silver came toward them. The Cloak batted it out of the air and Axiom-man hit it a second time on its decent to the floor.

Two more birds came in, one from either side. Axiom-man swung and missed. The bird doubled back and went for him again. This time his strike struck pay dirt and the bird hit the floor. Axiom-man struck it a few more times before letting it lie.

The Crimson Cloak swung at the bird, misjudged his distance, and ended up hitting it with the back of his palm. The bird circled around and came at him again. He swung the baton and hit one of the bird's wings. He swung again, this time aiming for the head, smacked it, and the bird went down.

Silence hung on the air but not for long because a flurry of silver birds flew in from either side then came at them from the center. One clipped the Crimson Cloak's jaw, cutting him. Another nipped his cheek.

He swung the baton and knocked one out of the air. He swung again and hit another.

He was getting the hang of this.

———

Axiom-man again lamented the fact he didn't have his powers here. He could be shooting these birds from the air with the energy beams from his eyes. He could have also avoided being cut thanks to a thin aura of energy that normally covered his body.

He swung like a wild man, sometimes hitting the birds, sometimes not. He took a deep breath and decided to slow down, to focus.

A clip to his shoulder. More blood.

He smacked another bird from the air then another.

The party of birds was finally starting to thin.

He struck one bird, missed another, struck another one, missed another only for the Crimson Cloak to move closer to his side and hit it for him.

There were only two birds left.

Arms stinging from the cuts, Axiom-man took a swipe at one of the birds, missed, then swung his arm back, hitting it.

The Crimson Cloak hit the last one as if hitting a home run.

The two men stood there, catching their breath.

"We return to the elevator," the Cloak said but not before heavy footsteps made themselves known.

A bird-like humanoid figure emerged from the shadows. It was silver with silver wings and two metal talons for feet. Its face was beaked with silver metal feathers that ran up the side of its head for ears.

"Oh great," Axiom-man said.

The Crimson Cloak remained silent.

The bird man moved in then lashed out one of its clawed hands, narrowly missing Axiom-man. It let out a squawk and tried to strike the Crimson Cloak, who avoided the blow by jumping a step backward.

Once more, Axiom-man yearned for his powers. How was he supposed to fight this thing? Any attempt to punch it would break his hand or foot. The Crimson Cloak took a swing at it and nailed it in the jaw. Axiom-man glanced at the Cloak's gloves: they were armored.

Using his baton, Axiom-man came in with a shot of his own and struck the robotic bird man in the neck. Its head went slightly to the side then whipped back to center. With another squawk, the creature lashed out and struck Axiom-man in the shoulder. Axiom-man momentarily put his hand to it and knew there'd be a wicked bruise there later.

The Crimson Cloak punched the bird man in the chest. Just then the bird man flung out its metallic wings and brought the left side around front, striking the Crimson Cloak in the face. He stumbled back and blood ran from his nose.

Axiom-man took another swing at it with his baton, this time aiming for right behind the knee, hoping the blow would be sufficient in causing it to stumble. The baton simply vibrated from the impact of metal on metal. Axiom-man didn't care and wailed blow after blow against the creature. The Crimson Cloak did the same thing. The bird man folded both his wings in front of him like a guard then quickly flayed them out, knocking the two men onto the floor. They got up and came at him again, striking any surface they could find on the bird man.

With another squawk, the bird man rose a few feet in the air then came at Axiom-man. He gave him a shove and on Axiom-man's stumble, flung out both taloned feet and grabbed Axiom-man by the shoulders and flew him up into the air.

"Axiom-man!" the Crimson Cloak said.

"A little help," Axiom-man called back.

The Crimson Cloak reached behind his back then pulled out his grappling gun. He shot the grapple and it hooked onto the bird man's arm. The Cloak went airborne. He retracted the cable, bringing him face to face with the bird man. He delivered a few blows to the bird man's head, probably hoping to knock some circuits loose, but the bird man continued its ascent.

The bird man circled the aviary and punched to the Cloak's ribs. Axiom-man heard a bone snap. The man in red grunted loud and primal. He supposed the blow was too much for even the Crimson Cloak's well-armoured body to handle. He looked up at the Cloak, who was freeing his grapple from the bird man's arm.

"Hold onto my legs," the Cloak said.

Axiom-man reached up and grabbed an ankle with each hand and hung on for dear life.

Once the Crimson Cloak got his grapple free, he fished around inside the inner liner of his trench coat and produced what looked like a small gun. Axiom-man thought the Crimson Cloak was going to shoot it and his guess wasn't far off. A fine bright blue laser came to life and the Cloak dragged the beam along the bird man's neck. Sparks flew everywhere. While he was doing this, he shot the grapple to one of the rafters.

It latched on.

Bright blue sparks lit up the Crimson Cloak's face and shimmered off the bird man's body.

Soon, he removed the head and the bird man stopped mid-flight and began to fall.

"Hold on," the Crimson Cloak said.

Axiom-man clung on.

The bird man fell to the ground as the Crimson Cloak swung him and Axiom-man gently to the floor.

Axiom-man touched down first and let go of the Cloak's booted ankles. The Crimson Cloak landed beside him.

"Next time open with that," Axiom-man said.

The Crimson Cloak only grunted, then said, "Let's go."

As they headed toward the elevator, Axiom-man said, "We're walking right into another trap."

"If we are, we are. Eventually, this will end. This is not limitless."

The Crimson Cloak was right. Eventually this obstacle course would come to an end. The real question was would they survive it?

At the elevator, the Cloak pressed the call button.

A whooshing sound filled the room and a wave of water came barreling at them.

This time Axiom-man hit the call button. "Come on, come on." *No time to rest.*

Another wave, this one crashing into them. The water was already knee-deep. The ceiling came to life as sprinklers dispelled water, adding to the ever-growing depth at floor level.

The Crimson Cloak hit the call button again.

The water was at their chests.

Maybe this was it? Maybe whoever was behind this was done with them and was going to drown them?

The water rose and submerged the call button. Axiom-man pressed it.

Water at chin level, the door finally opened and liquid flooded the elevator. They swam in and Axiom-man noticed that just beneath the water line, the number 3 button was lit.

The door slid shut and the elevator ascended.

"Curiouser and curiouser," said the man in front of the monitors. "Let's see how they like Level Three."

CHAPTER SIX

THE CRIMSON CLOAK was growing impatient. He'd been through similar nonsense before on his other adventures, and he wished whoever was behind this would just show themselves.

The elevator came to an abrupt halt and the door opened, letting out the water. Both the Crimson Cloak and Axiom-man pressed against adjacent walls to prevent themselves from sliding out with the water.

"How about we try *not* getting out of the elevator," Axiom-man said.

"Agreed," the Cloak replied.

The two stood there and waited . . . and waited.

A flash of heat washed over the Crimson Cloak's face. He looked up and metal coils rimmed the elevator's walls, burning a bright red. Axiom-man must have seen him looking up because he looked up too. Still, they stood there, testing the heat.

Axiom-man adjusted his mask. "I'm sweating."

"Try wearing several layers of dense fabric."

The heat was too much. Clearly, whoever was behind this wanted them out of the elevator. So much for that idea.

They stepped out and cool, fresh air rushed over them. They took a moment to take in their surroundings.

"This is the weirdest hotel I've ever been in," Axiom-man said.

The Crimson Cloak nodded his agreement.

The elevator door slid shut behind them.

The room was filled with trees and bushes and foliage. About ten feet to either side of them were woodchip paths. They presumably went around the room in a horseshoe shape.

"Left or right," Axiom-man said.

"Left."

"Reason?"

"None. Just a gut feeling."

The two men made their way to the path on the left. The fresh scent of greenery greeted the Crimson Cloak's nostrils even through his respirator. They moved slowly down the path, the Cloak on guard the whole time. He scanned the surrounding bushes and the trees mixed in with them. In the center of the room was a large oak with gnarled branches that almost reached the ceiling. He noticed Axiom-man looking at it as they walked.

"I'm going up top, see if I can get a bird's eye view," Axiom-man said.

"Be careful."

———

Axiom-man nodded and made his way through the bush to the base of the big tree. Its first thick branch was about a foot above his head. He jumped, grabbed onto the branch, then pulled himself up and got on top of it. There were more climbing branches. He made his ascent. Almost to the top and already he saw the whole of the room. Nothing but forest.

"Looks all clear from up here," Axiom-man shouted down to the Crimson Cloak.

But deep down he knew it wasn't all clear. None of the rooms they'd been in were all clear. Something was in here with them. One thing or more, he didn't know. He just had the foreboding feeling they weren't alone.

He checked for cameras but didn't see any. Whoever was behind this went to an awful lot of trouble to make each level a challenge.

"I'm coming down," Axiom-man said.

Just as he let go of the branch he held onto, the whole tree began to sway, at first side to side then front to back.

"Axiom-man!" the Crimson Cloak shouted from below.

"I'm okay. I'm—" Before he could finish speaking, a thick tree branch wrapped around him, pinning his arms to his body. He tried to resist and free himself but to no avail. He kicked his legs, hoping the jerking motion of his body would set him loose. It didn't. Another branch came in from the side and pinned his feet together, binding him to the tree.

If only he had his ultra strength. If only he knew why in this world he didn't have his powers.

He cleared his throat. "Help!"

———

The Crimson Cloak weaved through the bushes and got to the base of the tree. Axiom-man was about twenty feet up.

"Hang on," he said.

He heard a grinding noise and looked up to see the branches tightening against Axiom-man. He began to ascend. A lower branch wrapped around his ankle, stopping him. He tried to kick his leg free but the thing had grabbed him good. Another branch came in from the side, wrapping itself around the Cloak's arms and chest.

He had to think.

The laser cutter.

He reached into his cloak and pulled it out and got straight to work on cutting the branch around his chest and arms. As he cut through, he noticed he wasn't cutting wood but metal. This tree was mechanical, artificial. Not real.

He cut through then grabbed a branch for balance. It coiled around his wrist. He grabbed the laser cutter from the bound hand and leaned down and freed his legs. He then freed his wrist and double-timed it up the tree.

He got to Axiom-man and cut him loose.

Another tree branch tried to wrap itself around them but they leaned back and it missed.

"Hold on," the Crimson Cloak said and grabbed one side of his cape and wrapped it around Axiom-man's shoulders. He then grabbed the other side of his cape and pushed off from the tree and crudely parachuted down to the ground. Once they touched the woodchip path, he took his arm off Axiom-man's shoulder.

"Thanks," Axiom-man said.

"Don't mention it."

"Let's get out of here."

"Agreed."

They headed toward the elevator. A sickening feeling filled the Crimson Cloak's stomach this was not over.

Not yet.

———

At the elevator, Axiom-man hit the call button. "I wonder what's next?"

The Crimson Cloak pointed to the trail on the right. "That."

It emerged from the foliage, a woman made of wood or wearing a wooden suit. Her face was covered in bark as were her forearms and shins. No, it couldn't be a wooden suit. She moved toward them with fluidity and formed a grimace on her face, something impossible if it was a mere mask.

The wooden woman let out a screech and charged at Axiom-man. She swung. He ducked. She came in with a kick to the thigh. It was like getting hit with a baseball bat and Axiom-man dropped to one knee. She delivered a right hook and Axiom-man's world flipped upside down and backward from the blow.

She moved to hit him again but a black glove stopped her.

The Crimson Cloak.

Axiom-man was thankful for the Cloak's arm guards and what appeared to be hard rubber-coated knuckles.

The Cloak blocked another blow and did a jumping side kick to the wooden woman's middle. She let out a screech again, raspy and strong.

Axiom-man got up and wobbled on his leg for a moment before grabbing the wooden woman from behind in an attempted choke hold . . . except there was nothing soft to squeeze. Her neck was as solid as her body. Didn't matter. If he couldn't punch her due to his gloves being made of fabric, he was going to wrestle her instead and let the Crimson Cloak apply the force needed to subdue her.

The Cloak kicked the woman in the face with his heavy boot. Axiom-man assumed they were steel-toed because he heard a crack. Axiom-man reached for the bark on the woman's forearm to see if he could peel it away but it wouldn't budge. The woman took advantage of Axiom-man's free hand and got out of the choke hold. Head still spinning from the previous blow, Axiom-man suddenly saw a flash of black then a flash of green stars as she socked him in the head once again. The headache that formed was so strong he found it difficult to see.

The Crimson Cloak leveled a spinning turning kick across the woman's face then zoomed in and pummeled her in the gut with his fists. The woman struck the Crimson Cloak in the face. A bruise almost immediately appeared on his cheekbone. The Cloak dropped to the floor and intertwined his legs with the woman's. He twisted his hips and swept her legs out from under her. She hit the floor with a hard, sickening smack. Axiom-man got behind her and put her in another choke hold, the idea being to stop her from flailing around and give the Crimson Cloak an easy target. The Cloak must have taken the cue because he went for her head once more and punched and punched and punched. The woman kicked out a turning kick, getting the ball of her foot around and rammed her foot into the Crimson Cloak's back, sending him forward so he was face to face with her. She screeched again. Axiom-man pulled and sat her more upright and locked his legs around her. She struggled against his hold and for a brief moment Axiom-man thought she was going to get loose. The Crimson Cloak stood and kicked her in the head. She kicked him in the shin but it didn't matter against what Axiom-man guessed were armored boots.

The woman wriggled and writhed, loosening herself from Axiom-man's grip. She cocked an elbow and nailed him in the throat. Coughing, trying to get some air, Axiom-man's world spun when he suddenly found himself flat on his face against the floor. By the time he rolled over, both the woman and the Crimson Cloak stood toe-to-toe. She took a swing at him. He leaned back, causing her to miss. He kicked the underside of her chin, then slid in sideways, grabbing her by the arm and tossing her over his hip to the floor.

Axiom-man got to his feet, head swimming, and through blurry vision, found his target. He jumped up and landed on her chest. He stomped down on her several times before she grabbed his foot, twisted it at the ankle, and he stumbled off of her. She got in behind the Crimson Cloak. He spun and swung at her but missed when she moved her head to the side. He then blurted to Axiom-man, "Get back!"

Axiom-man obeyed. The Cloak took two giant steps backward. The woman charged him. He sent her flying backward with a push kick then grabbed Axiom-man by the shoulder and pulled him further away.

"What—?" Axiom-man started then noticed a small silver device on the woman's chest. He looked to the Crimson Cloak, who held a black rectangle in his palm.

Before Axiom-man could say another word, the Crimson Cloak pressed a button on the rectangle. The woman's chest blew open, leaving a wide gaping hole. She dropped to her knees then fell face first to the floor.

"Why do you always save your tricks for the end?" Axiom-man asked.

"Because I try and deal with threats as humanely as possible before going to last resorts."

The elevator door slid open. They both looked at the exit.

"What if we don't go in and just stay here? Then whoever's behind this won't be able to throw any more surprises at us?" Axiom-man said.

"Then we wait."

The two stood there not saying anything, Axiom-man too busy trying to keep the nausea at bay from the blows to his head. What felt like a migraine started to set in.

"You wouldn't happen to have any painkillers on you, would you?" Axiom-man asked.

"Here." The Crimson Cloak reached into his coat and pulled out a small vial. "This is concentrated painkiller. Will clear your head."

Axiom-man took the vial and sucked it back. The moment he was done, smoke began to fill the room, thick and dark with a sharp smell, like burning wire. The smoke grew so thick Axiom-man could hardly see.

"To the elevator," the Crimson Cloak said.

"Oh joy," Axiom-man said.

They made their way to the elevator and got in. The door slid shut.

Axiom-man studied the panel of buttons. One with the letter R lit up and the elevator began to move.

———

The figure looked at the monitor showing the two caped men in the elevator.

"Surely there's no time to rest as these boys complete my test. It will end in victory or defeat but either way this has been a glorious treat."

The figure crossed his arms and leaned back in his chair. "One more show to go, neither fast neither slow."

CHAPTER SEVEN

THE ELEVATOR DOOR slid open and the two caped crusaders stepped out onto the roof.

The Crimson Cloak wished he could say it was over, that this . . . trial . . . had been passed, but he knew better than to count his blessings. Too many fights, too many battles against bad guys taught him they didn't give up and kept attacking until the war was over.

The two proceeded with caution farther onto the roof. It was bare except for some air ducts, which seemed out of place.

"Something doesn't feel right," Axiom-man said.

"Agreed," the Crimson Cloak replied.

The two stood there a moment. There was something on the air but the Crimson Cloak couldn't quite place it. He reached for his grappling gun, pulled it out and made his way to the roof's ledge. He peered over it. They were about four storeys up and, upon a quick glance, around thirteen blocks from the alley where they were gassed.

Axiom-man must have slid in beside him unnoticed because the Cloak caught him in his peripheral. Good. He was stealthy.

"I used to be able to fly," Axiom-man said.

"Really." It was more a statement than a question.

"But I can't here. Your world—I don't have my powers."

"What can you do, anyway?"

"I'm strong. Real strong. I can fly and shoot energy beams from my eyes. I also have this faint aura that covers me and grants limited protection against attacks. A knife, for example. But in your world, yeah, all gone."

"Those powers could have come in handy tonight."

"Tell me about it."

The Crimson Cloak aimed his grapple gun at the streetlamp below. He fired. The line and grapple went out and struck something two feet away then went limp. It struck . . . nothing.

"What the—" the Crimson Cloak said. He hopped up on the ledge and reached out. He recoiled his hand when a shot of what felt like electricity zapped his fingers.

Axiom-man reached out as well and had the same result.

The Cloak marched to an adjacent ledge and reached out again. His fingers ached from another zap.

Frustrated, he aimed his grapple upward and pulled the trigger. The grapple went straight up about thirty feet then hit the invisible barrier and fell to the ground. The Crimson Cloak retracted the cord and put the grappling gun back on his belt.

"Trapped," Axiom-man said.

"This fight isn't over."

The two men stood in silence, the Cloak assuming Axiom-man was trying to work out his next move.

"The only thing I can think of is going back to the elevator and seeing if we can ride it down to the main floor," Axiom-man said.

"That floor was engulfed in flame, remember?"

"Oh yeah. Maybe the fire's died out?"

"Doubt it." He paused for a moment and thought. "The common denominator to all this is indeed that elevator." He walked past Axiom-man and headed toward it. When he was about twenty feet away, the elevator door slid open. Immediately its occupant stepped out onto the roof.

The Crimson Cloak stopped in his tracks. Axiom-man caught up from behind.

Before them stood a giant of man, at least nine feet tall and as wide as two men standing beside each other. He wore a white tank top and ripped black pants. His muscles were covered with veins straining to break through the skin, and his face—it was like two halves from two different faces glued together. One eye was lower than the other. The bridge of his nose was wide and had a kind of diamond shape akin to a healed broken nose. Thick lips drew back to reveal yellow teeth. His brown hair was a mess. If anyone was hired muscle, it was this guy.

The Crimson Cloak had been right: This fight was far from over.

Adrenaline dumped into Axiom-man's system, filling him with energy but also making his legs a bit wobbly. Normally, this kind of thing wouldn't faze him but without his powers, he felt helpless. Still, he had come this far without his abilities and he wasn't going to give up now.

He looked to the Crimson Cloak, who remained as stoic as ever, as if he'd done this a million times before. If the guy was frightened by the menace in front of them, he didn't show it. All he showed was a firm jawline that no doubt held gritted teeth beneath that respirator of his.

The . . . mutant . . . didn't waste any time and a big, meaty hand came crashing in from the side, landing bang on into Axiom-man's jaw. His head turned from the blow and he heard—and felt—his neck go out of place as darkness rimmed his vision. Head spinning, he managed to duck the next strike. He gave his neck a crack, realigning things, then moved in close to the mutant and wailed on its mid-section with everything he had.

The Crimson Cloak kicked the mutant in the knees, both in the front and in the back. The mutant's long arm swatted him away like a fly, sending him flying into the air ducts some ten feet away.

Axiom-man punched and punched, his fists pummeling the mutant in the ribs. It was like hitting a wall of dense meat. The creature picked him up by the shoulders and held him in front of him. Axiom-man kicked the mutant in the head and in the neck, hoping against hope he was doing some damage but each blow didn't seem to faze the mutant. The next thing Axiom-man knew, he flew through the air and crashed into the air ducts as well, their sharp corners digging into his back. Thankfully, his cape and uniform were thick enough to stop the corner of the unit from cutting him.

He looked to the Crimson Cloak. "You okay?"

The Cloak nodded, got up, took a moment's pause, then ran at the creature. Axiom-man got to his feet, his head still spinning. In front of him on what felt like a tilting rooftop, the Crimson Cloak hammered away at the mutant's stomach and chest, kicking and punching it. The mutant grabbed the Cloak by the neck and lifted him up. Axiom-man ran over and brought both fists down on the mutant's forearm, forcing the mutant to drop the Crimson Cloak. Another swat, this time catching Axiom-man in the shoulder and sending him flying into the rooftop's ledge.

Come on. Get up, Axiom-man thought. "Get. Up." He shakily got to his feet, took a moment to let the world stop spinning, then ran back to the action.

The Crimson Cloak flung a front kick to the mutant's thigh then lifted his leg even higher and threw another front kick under the mutant's chin with the same leg. The mutant's head snapped back from the blow. When it reaffixed its eyes on the Crimson Cloak, they were filled with fury. The Cloak delivered a solid right hook, then a left, then a right, then a left, the mutant's head snapping to the side with each strike.

The mutant kicked the Crimson Cloak in the gut. He doubled over and nausea filled his entire being.

Out of the corner of his eye, he caught Axiom-man pummeling the mutant in the kidneys. The mutant kicked Axiom-man to the side. Axiom-man rebounded and kicked the mutant in the back of the knee, taking its leg out from under it. The mutant momentarily got down on one knee from the kick. The Crimson Cloak punched it square in the face before being swatted to the side.

The mutant threw Axiom-man into the air ducts again and the thing lumbered toward him. The Crimson Cloak ran at the mutant full tilt and did a flying side kick into the mutant's neck, forcing it to stop moving. The Cloak kicked at the mutant's back then punched it in the back of the head.

The mutant straightened, looked to the Crimson Cloak, and delivered a right hook to the Cloak's temple. Immediately, the Crimson Cloak dropped to his knees, his legs suddenly turning to rubber. Blackness rimmed his vision and little green stars shimmered in his line of sight.

This wasn't working. They were getting nowhere.

Axiom-man sailed through the air again and skidded across the roof, crashing into the elevator's door.

Only brute force could take this creature down and it seemed the combined strength of the Crimson Cloak and Axiom-man wasn't enough. It was time to use some smarts. The Cloak thought for a moment then had an idea.

With a splitting headache, he stood on shaky legs. He reached for his grapple gun. Once in hand, he fired it at the mutant. The grapple plowed into the mutant's chest and it wavered. The Crimson Cloak retracted the line and just as he was about to do it again, the mutant charged him and ran him over. Now on his back, head throbbing, his eyes wanting to close, the Cloak thought hard about what to do.

He looked to the mutant. The mutant held Axiom-man by the neck, the man in the blue cape kicking the mutant in the head.

Neck.

Head.

The Crimson Cloak holstered his grapple gun and reached farther across the inside of his cloak and pulled out a set of bolas.

Axiom-man was slammed face down on the rooftop.

The Crimson Cloak sturdied his legs beneath him as best he could, took a moment to focus and rode a wave of dizziness. Once it passed, he spun the bolas in his right hand then hurled them at the mutant. The bolas wrapped around the mutant's neck. Just as the mutant reached for them, the Crimson Cloak jumped on its back and grabbed the bolas and pulled, tightening the rope around the mutant's neck like a noose. He held on for dear life as the mutant twisted and turned, trying to shake him off. The Crimson Cloak only held onto the bolas even harder, pulling them as tight as he could.

The mutant reached up and grabbed the Cloak by the head. A hand now covering his line of sight, he shook his head, trying to free it from the mutant's grip. He did. And he squeezed.

And squeezed.

And squeezed.

The mutant fell onto one knee then the other. Axiom-man stood before it and delivered a left hook to the mutant's head then a right then a left.

"Keep hitting him," the Crimson Cloak said.

Axiom-man did, striking the mutant in the temples.

The Cloak started to dip forward with the mutant, the bolas around its neck doing their job, cutting off blood to the brain. The Cloak held on. Axiom-man kept striking.

Finally, the mutant keeled over. Even with the Crimson Cloak now lying on top of him, he still held the bolas good and firm, ensuring the mutant was indeed passed out.

Once he was sure the mutant was unconscious, he loosened his grip only a little. Then a little bit more. Then a little bit more.

Axiom-man stomped on the back of the mutant's head for good measure.

It was over.

Finally.

———

The Crimson Cloak rose to his feet. Axiom-man helped steady him. Both men just stood there, catching their breath, waiting for something to happen to get them off the roof and back into the elevator but . . . nothing occurred.

Slow clapping arose on the air and both men turned around to see a short man wearing blue dress pants and a white button-up shirt under a red sweater. He had dirty blond hair and part of his face was hidden behind a pair of square-framed sunglasses that reflected the night.

"Bravo, bravo, you pair of heroes," the man said. "You made it through my trial filled with bloody style. Now here you are upon my roof, keenly aware and not aloof."

"Who are you?" Axiom-man asked. If this was the guy that truly put him and the Crimson Cloak through the obstacle course, the man better damn well identify himself.

"You can call me the Trial Master," the man said.

"Why the trials?" the Crimson Cloak asked.

"Oh, wouldn't you like to know whether I answer swiftly or answer slow. You are part of a much bigger game, some parts different, some parts the same."

The Crimson Cloak stepped closer to the man. So did Axiom-man.

"Don't come any closer until I finish speaking for it is in my words the meaning you're seeking." The man put his hands behind his back. Axiom-man got ready in case the man was going to pull out a weapon. Instead, the man just stood there.

"Life is about growth and care. The problem is you can't find those things everywhere. But in my trial you found growth and for that you owe me as you can plainly see."

Wish this guy would stop monologuing, Axiom-man thought.

"You two are part of a much bigger plan, the question was if you can. And, boy, did you succeed, namely out of need. But I'm thoroughly impressed you made it through Phase One and boy oh boy was it fun."

"Phase One?" Axiom-man asked.

"Yes, the first phase of two. This one is complete but there is more for you. Not now, not tonight. Get your rest so you can fight. All at the appropriate time, of course, and I'll be there right at the source."

"I don't have time for this," the Crimson Cloak muttered. He moved toward the man and went to grab him at the shoulders. The Cloak's hands passed through the man, encompassing nothing but air.

"Be seeing you in Phase Two," the man said then vanished.

There was a flicker of blue light all around the roof. Axiom-man assumed it was the force field going down. He stepped up on the building's ledge and reached out, connecting with nothing but air.

"I don't like what that guy said," Axiom-man said.

"I don't either," the Crimson Cloak replied.

"I'm not even from here. Does he know something I don't? That I'll somehow return to this world at a later date?"

The Crimson Cloak stroked his chin then said, "I don't know. What I do know is you need to go home, and we need to figure out how to do that."

Axiom-man thought a moment then said, "Let's get back to that alley."

"I need to go there anyway to make sure the guy was picked up by the police."

"Then let's go."

Chapter Eight

When they got to the alley, the Crimson Cloak was relieved to see the man he left tied up was gone as was the little girl. He'd have to follow up with the police to make sure she was safe.

Axiom-man was close to the mouth of the alley, moving his hands around in the air as if searching for something.

"What are you doing?" the Crimson Cloak asked.

"Trying to find the thin spot."

The Cloak thought long and hard while Axiom-man searched. Something obviously triggered the thin spot and brought Axiom-man through.

"Normally, these thin spots are marked by black clouds, like a vertical line of deep dark smoke on the air," Axiom-man said. "There's nothing here and I need to go home. My city needs me."

"There might be a way," the Crimson Cloak said, "but I'm not sure it will work."

"Yeah? How?"

"My red gas." He pointed to his respirator. "I think it brought you here, somehow mixed with your thin spot and got you here."

Axiom-man moved his hand up and down through the air. "I think this is where the thin spot is. Can you spray it with that gas?"

The Crimson Cloak shook his head. "It doesn't work that way. You need to be in the thick of it."

Axiom-man was silent for a moment, as if thinking. "Then that's what we'll do."

"The red gas is no joke. You will relive past pain and all your fears will become manifest."

"If that's what it takes to get me home, so be it."

The Crimson Cloak released a heavy sigh. "Are you sure about this?"

"I'm sure."

The Crimson Cloak moved closer to Axiom-man. "Before we do this, thank you for the help tonight."

"No, thank you for *your* help tonight. It's been an honor to serve with you." He stuck out his hand for a handshake.

The Crimson Cloak took it and shook it. "Now just relax and look right here." He pointed to his respirator.

———

The world went murky red and encompassed Axiom-man's entire field of vision. He tried closing his eyes but that didn't work. The red gas stung through his eyelids.

Suddenly, he felt fourteen and called his dad a jerk. The word pierced him to his soul. How could a fourteen-year-old say that to a parent?

He was seventeen and he lied to his mom. His mom knew he was lying, and Axiom-man felt the sting of the betrayal. His heart went hollow.

He was a kid and was rough housing with his brother. Things got out of hand, and he punched his brother in the face. Axiom-man felt that punch.

He was in school doing a math test and he peeked over at the person next to his desk, trying to see the answer to question 17. He was the person writing the test and he felt the awkwardness of knowing somebody was cheating.

A black fist appeared then struck him in the face. Blood gushed from his nose. "You will die." It was Redsaw.

All went completely dark. "My world." It was Bleaken.

"Mike, I'm dead. Or maybe not." Katie.

"Save me! Gabriel, help!" Valerie!

Axiom-man was on his knees.

"You will let us die." He didn't recognize the voice but had the impression it was the entire city accusing him of a crime he didn't commit.

"Failure." The messenger. "I chose wrong."

His head abuzz with memories, the red mist grew thinner and thinner until the gas was no more, and he was in an alley. A different alley.

The Crimson Cloak was gone.

Catching his breath, he waited a moment on his knees before standing. He felt stronger. He looked at his hand and saw the feint aura of his powers.

"Good bye, my friend," he said. He looked up. It was nearing dawn.

Axiom-man floated into the sky and headed for home.

———

Axiom-man faded away and the Crimson Cloak could only assume that it worked, and his partner returned to his own world.

He thought back to the Trial Master and the warning of Phase Two. Whatever Phase Two was, the Crimson Cloak vowed to stop it.

The sun was slowly coming up.

The Crimson Cloak pulled out his grapple gun and shot the grapple to the nearest rooftop.

It was time to go home.

CHAPTER NINE

SOMETHING HAD TO be done. Axiom-man didn't know what or how, but the Doorway had left nothing but destruction in its wake. If it wasn't for that horrible night with Redsaw, if it wasn't for all that black smoke and cloud, if it wasn't for entering some endless strange realm of red and black, nothing that had happened since would have happened.

Axiom-man was there. He saw the Doorway. Deep inside, he knew he fought with all he had with all the power he had at the time. He did everything possible to seal the Doorway and protect those who were caught in the crossfire.

He had given it his all.

Now, more powerful than he was back then, he couldn't help but think if he could have done more. Perhaps a Surge could have occurred. But Surges weren't up to him. They were up to the messenger. A Surge only happened when he had proven himself worthy of the current power he had. So far, it seemed, he had done well enough with what he was given because a few Surges had occurred since he first got his powers, but at the time of the Doorway, he wasn't where he was at now.

A rock filled his stomach and his heart ached. *It's not your fault. You were up against something way more powerful than you. Up against someone who was more powerful than you.* That someone was Redsaw and ever since Axiom-man had embarked on his crusade, Redsaw was always there in the shadows, coming out just when Axiom-man felt like he had a handle on things.

The Doorway of Darkness. He knew it was tied to Redsaw. Redsaw created the portal to begin with, after all. But how deeply enmeshed they were, Axiom-man didn't know.

Clearly, the Doorway was more than just a portal to another dimension. Its residual clouds acted as their own doorways to other places. Now, Axiom-man learned after being with the Crimson Cloak, it was also a doorway through . . . . He realized where he had been: Old town Winnipeg. Either the 1910s or '20s, maybe. But he'd never heard of the Crimson Cloak. Did the Doorway, the thin spot, take him to the past?

Axiom-man paused mid-flight and hovered above the city. If that was true, that could mean there were black clouds scattered throughout history, possibly even the future. And there was no way to pinpoint them. No way to track them down and try and close them off. They were just . . . everywhere.

You should have done a better job sealing the Doorway, he thought. "No . . . there's nothing more you could have done at the time," he said softly. He was so used to winning, so used to defeating the bad guys that this defeat—because that's what it was—was different. This was a loss against something he couldn't hit or couldn't blast with his eye beams. No physical intervention could ever put the Doorway in its place and stop its effects forever. *What do you do when you can't win?*

Axiom-man flew on. It was time to go home. Time to see Valerie. Time to fall into her arms and for the moments she held him, forget the world.

Forget the Doorway.

Forget the Crimson Cloak.

Forget it all.

CHAPTER TEN

THE CRIMSON CLOAK stood over the city. He furrowed his brow and clenched his jaw at the thought that he was no longer this world's sole protector. Protecting the city, going elsewhere when needed—that was all he knew. But now, he knew there was someone else. Someone who defied the laws of physics and came here to his city. The Crimson Cloak was not a scientist. Sure, he understood chemistry fairly well hence his red gas, but other sciences—no, they weren't studied nor cared for. They never seemed needed. A little biology, sure, understanding the human body and how it worked and the best places to strike, but that's about as far as he took his biological studies. It was about combat. About having an edge over his opponents. But how can he now have an edge over someone who could travel through time, if that's what indeed happened? What kind of power was there that enabled that? Clearly the Trial Master had access to—or even created—mechanical inventions that were unheard of.

It was then the Crimson Cloak's heart sunk and his stomach churned. He was just a human in a detective suit and a mask trying to make a difference.

He was just a human.

Human.

Nothing more, nothing less.

No matter how hard he had tried to perfect his body and sharpen his mind in the ways he felt important . . . none of it would be good enough now. Not with this knowledge. Not with knowing that Axiom-man was out there albeit in a different time.

The world opened up. It was no longer countries and land divisions and cities. That was the present. That was the world as it was right here, right now. But the Earth had existed long before the Crimson Cloak came into being, and it would exist long after he was gone. The world was no longer constrained by time. It was just World.

Earth.

History, the present, the future—all of it—was Earth.

The Crimson Cloak got down on one knee and said a prayer. *Lord, there is no way for me to fully understand this. But You do. Show me what to do next.*

He rose and let the wind billow his long red cape around him. The flapping then settling of the fabric cocooned him and, for a moment, he felt back in the present, back where he belonged.

"Never forget," he said. "This is now. Should the past come, it is welcome. Should the future return, it is welcome as well." *Your job is here. Now. Tonight.*

He took a deep breath and let the oxygen replenish his energy.

Gun shots, three alleys over.

The Crimson Cloak turned and ran across the rooftop, leaping to the next, heading to where he belonged.

Right here.

Right now.

Earth.

About the Author

A.P. Fuchs is the author of many novels and short stories. His most recent books are *Zomtropolis: A Record of Life in a Dead City*, *Giganti-gator Death Machine: Triple Feature*, and *Axiom-man/Auroraman: Frozen Storm*.

Also a cartoonist, he is known for his superhero series, *The Axiom-man Saga*, both in novel and comic book format. Please visit **www.canisterx.com** for more on this series. For his webcomic, *Fredrikus*, about a down-and-out anthropomorphic dog in a dystopian sci-fi world, please go to **www.fredrikus.com**

As well, be sure to subscribe to A.P. Fuchs's YouTube Channel at **www.youtube.com/@apfuchs** for books, comics, podcasts, stories, and more.

www.ingramcontent.com/pod-product-compliance
Lightning Source LLC
Chambersburg PA
CBHW031257210726
48287CB00003B/1070